Rebus Treasury II

Compiled by the editors
of Highlights for Children

BOYDS MILLS PRESS

Copyright © 1993 by Boyds Mills Press
All rights reserved

Published by Bell Books
Boyds Mills Press, Inc.
A Highlights Company
815 Church Street
Honesdale, Pennsylvania 18431
Printed in the United States of America

Publisher Cataloging-in-Publication Data
   Rebus treasury II : forty-four stories kids can read by following the
pictures / compiled by the editors of Highlights for Children.—1st ed.
[48]p. : col. ill. ; cm.
Originally published in *Highlights for Children.*
ISBN 1-56397-063-5
1. Rebuses—Juvenile literature. [1. Rebuses.] I. Title.
   [E]—dc20   1993   CIP/AC
Library of Congress Catalog Card Number 92-75882

First edition, 1993
Book designed by Charlie Cary
The text of this book is set in 14-point Century Schoolbook.
Distributed by St. Martin's Press

10 9 8 7 6 5 4 3

Cover art by Marion Krupp

Contents

Reading a Rebus

Right from the start, your young child can delight in reading these rebus stories simply by identifying the little pictures. Each picture is followed by the word it represents, so your child will become familiar with the words while enjoying successful reading.

As you read these stories aloud, you may want to encourage your child to point to the pictures. Learning to follow a story by moving from left to right gives a child an important head start on the road to good reading.

We hope that the stories in this book will provide hours of family fun and help your child become a skilled, enthusiastic reader.

Tina's Trip

By Clare Mishica
Illustrated by Ethel Gold

 Tina put on a spacesuit and climbed into her

 spaceship. The engines roared. 3, 2, 1, Blast-off!

Her spaceship headed for the ◯ Moon.

 Tina looked out her  window at the stars. She

looked down at the Earth. The Earth was as small as

a beach ball.

Bump, bump, bump. Tina landed in a giant crater on

the ◯ Moon. She climbed out of her spaceship to explore. She

heard strange noises behind a big rock. Suddenly a furry space

creature with a long, red tongue jumped out and licked her.

 Tina jumped into her spaceship. 3, 2, 1, Blast-off!

Back to Earth she went.

Tina's mother was waiting for her when she landed.

"Jump out of that box now," she said. "Let's pick up toys,

and after that we can take Ruffy for a walk."

"OK," Tina said. "Ruff, ruff," said the creature with the

long, red tongue.

Peekaboo Rabbits

By Ruth A. Sakri

Illustrated by Jan Pyk

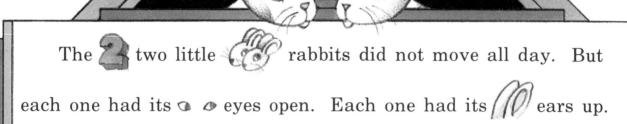

The 2 two little rabbits did not move all day. But each one had its eyes open. Each one had its ears up.

A cat walked by. Her paw almost touched the 2 two little rabbits. But they did not move, and the cat went away, pit-pat.

A dog walked by. His long tail almost touched the 2 two little rabbits. But they did not move, and the dog went away, wig-wag.

Then 2 two shoes walked by. The rabbits did not move, but the shoes stopped. 2 Two hands reached down and picked up the rabbits.

"Peekaboo!" said Becky. "I see you under my bed."

Becky dropped her shoes beside the bed. She put her feet into her slippers. At last the 2 two little rabbits began to move, flip-flop, hip-hop.

6

Words, Words, Words

By Judith Ross Enderle

Illustrated by Carol Sutherby

"Let's read a  book," said Duck.

"We don't have a book," said Frog.

"A boy left a book by the pond," said Duck. Rabbit, Duck, and Frog went to the pond.

There was a book by the hollow log.

"How do you read a book?" asked Frog.

"You open the book and say words," said Rabbit.

"I can do that," said Frog.

"Me, too," said Duck. Rabbit opened the book.

"Words, words, words," said Rabbit, Duck, and Frog. "Words, words, words."

"When do we get to the story?" asked Frog.

"Soon," said Rabbit.

But they never did.

Fred, the Brave Dog

By Dawn Abraham

Illustrated by Marion Krupp

 Fred was very brave. He chased birds. He chased the cat. He barked at the moon and stars.

One day when Fred was playing with his  bone and his ball, the clouds hid the sun. The sky turned 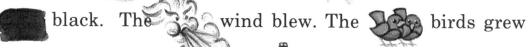 black. The wind blew. The birds grew quiet. The cat went into the house.

 Lightning flashed. Thunder crashed like a drum.

 Fred was afraid. He ran into the house and crawled under the bed.

After a while the moon and stars came out. But Fred stayed under the  bed.

When the sun came up the next day, Fred went outside. He found his bone and his ball. He even chased the cat. Fred wasn't afraid anymore. He was still a brave dog. Even a brave dog can be afraid sometimes.

Front-Porch Mystery

By Judith Ross Enderle
Illustrated by Olivia H.H. Cole

Janet and Jack were playing checkers. They heard a noise. "Listen," said 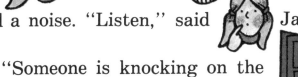 Janet. "What is that noise?"

"Someone is knocking on the  door," Jack said. He opened the door. But there was no one there—only their dog, sitting on the front 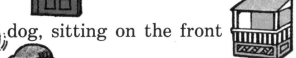 porch. He was wagging his tail. Jack sat down at the table again.

"Knock! Knock! Knock!"

"Someone is knocking on the door again," said Jack. "But when I looked, no one was there."

"Could it be someone playing a trick?" asked Janet.

 Janet and Jack tiptoed to the window. They looked out. But they could not see anyone.

Suddenly they heard, "Knock! Knock! Knock!" again.

They saw the 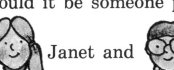 dog scratching his ear. Every time he scratched his ear, his leg hit the side of the  house.

Janet and Jack laughed.

City Breakfast

By Bruce Winter

Illustrated by Olivia H.H. Cole

Avi was visiting Grandma at her apartment in New York City.

"Time for a breakfast walk," Grandma called. They rode down in an elevator.

"Are we going to a restaurant?" Avi asked.

"This is called a deli," Grandma said as they went into a store.

They bought bagels and cream cheese. Grandma and Avi walked to the fruit stand at the corner.

"The fruit is good here," Grandma said. They bought a banana and an apple.

On the way home Grandma and Avi bought orange juice from a pushcart.

"Mm," said Avi. "I like taking a breakfast walk."

Country Breakfast

By Sandra Steen and Susan Steen

Illustrated by Meryl Henderson

 Amy was visiting Grandpa at his farm.

"It's time to get our breakfast," Grandpa called.

 Amy and Grandpa gathered eggs from the chickens.

 Amy asked, "Are we having eggs?"

"It is a surprise," Grandpa said.

They went to milk the 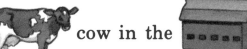 cow in the barn.

 Amy asked, "Are we having milk?"

"It is a surprise," Grandpa said.

They went to the garden and picked blueberries.

 Amy asked, "Are we having blueberries?"

"It is a surprise," Grandpa said.

They went to the kitchen. Grandpa mixed the eggs and milk and blueberries with flour and baking powder.

"Blueberry  pancakes!" Amy said. "I like my breakfast surprise."

Tabitha Builds a House

By Jacqueline Vickerstaff

Illustrated by Ethel Gold

"I am building something," Tabitha told Robin.

Tabitha measured some wood with a ruler.

"Is it for Squirrel?" tweeted Robin.

"No, it is not for Squirrel." Tabitha cut the wood with a saw. "It is for someone who lays eggs."

"Is it for Spider?" tweeted Robin.

"No, it is not for Spider." Tabitha hammered some nails into the wood. "It is for someone who has wings."

"Is it for Butterfly?" tweeted Robin.

"No, it is not for Butterfly." Tabitha tapped in the last nail with her hammer. "It is for someone who has feathers." Tabitha hung the thing she had built on a branch. "This is not for Squirrel or Spider or Butterfly." She smiled at Robin. "This is a birdhouse for you."

The Good News

By Marilyn Kratz

Illustrated by Linda Weller

A March breeze whispered the good news to

a cloud filled with raindrops.

The raindrops pattered down and shared the

good news with a blossom on an apple tree.

A robin sitting in her nest overheard the

good news. She sang it to a bee buzzing by.

The bee spread the good news to every

dandelion on the hill.

The dandelions did not have to say a word.

They just smiled up at the sun with their happy golden

faces. Now everyone knows the good news—spring is here!

Ashley's Treasure

By Lois Szymanski

Illustrated by Linda Weller

 Ashley searched the grass in the park, looking for a special treasure.

On a leaf she saw a ladybug. Ashley stopped to watch it, but the ladybug was not the treasure she needed.

Next Ashley saw a butterfly sitting on a flower. The butterfly was pretty, but it was not the treasure Ashley needed.

 Ashley saw something bright by the creek. She wondered if it could be her treasure. But it was not. It was a shiny stone.

Then Ashley saw it! She scooped up the can and dropped it in her sack. Ashley smiled. The more treasure she found, the cleaner her park would become.

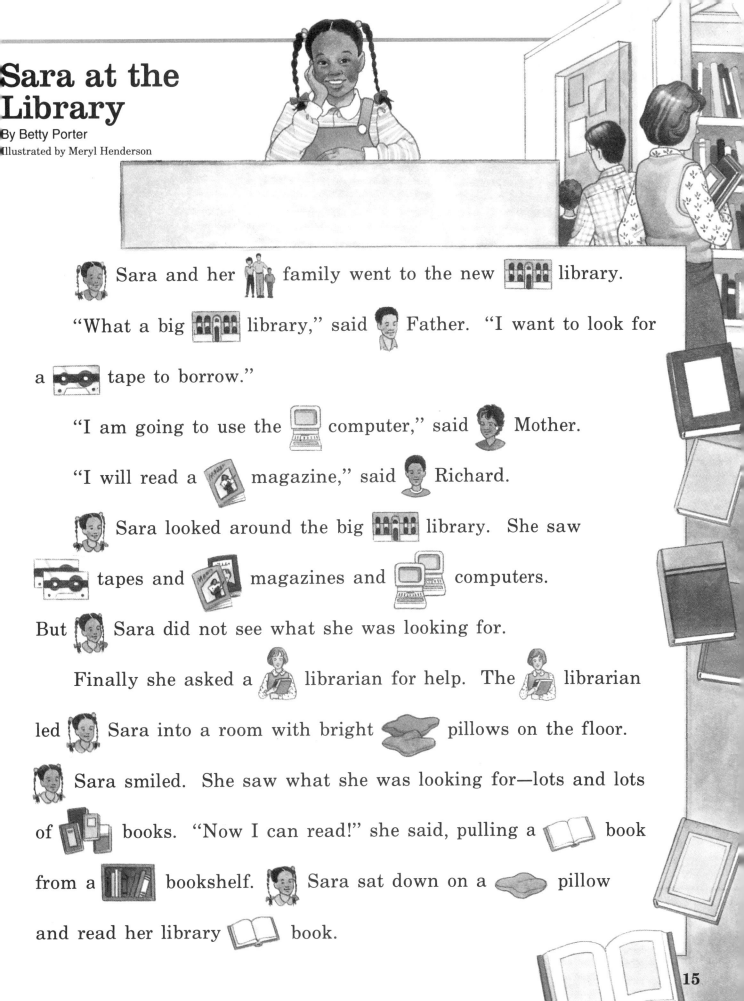

Sara at the Library

By Betty Porter

Illustrated by Meryl Henderson

Sara and her family went to the new library.

"What a big library," said Father. "I want to look for a tape to borrow."

"I am going to use the computer," said Mother.

"I will read a magazine," said Richard.

Sara looked around the big library. She saw tapes and magazines and computers. But Sara did not see what she was looking for.

Finally she asked a librarian for help. The librarian led Sara into a room with bright pillows on the floor.

Sara smiled. She saw what she was looking for—lots and lots of books. "Now I can read!" she said, pulling a book from a bookshelf. Sara sat down on a pillow and read her library book.

The Right Name

By Ruth A. Sakri

Illustrated by Meryl Henderson

 Ed watched four kittens playing in a box. They belonged to Mr. Young. "You may choose one," said Mr. Young to Ed.

 Ed smiled at the white kitten. He said, "I could name you Marshmallow." He touched the black kitten. "You could be Blackberry," he said. He petted the yellow kitten. "You could be Lemon Drop," he said. He stroked the orange kitten. "You could be Marmalade," he said.

 Mr. Young said, "Those are four sweet names. But you need five." He moved the box. Behind it sat another kitten. It was white, black, yellow, and orange.

"That is the kitten I want!" said Ed.

"OK," Mr. Young said. "But what will you name a kitten that comes in so many different colors?"

Ed hugged his kitten. "This is Jellybeans," he said.

16

The Most Important Thing

By Jacqueline Vickerstaff
Illustrated by Jan Pyk

 Erica frowned. "I think I forgot something at the

 pet store."

 Erica pulled a cage out of her shopping bag.

"My hamster will live in this cage." She put

a wheel inside the cage. "My hamster will run

on this wheel."

 Erica hung a bottle on the side of the cage.

"My hamster will drink from this bottle." She put

 seeds on the bottom of the cage. "My hamster

will eat these seeds."

 Erica scratched her head. "I remembered the cage.

I remembered the wheel. I remembered the bottle.

I remembered the seeds."

Suddenly Erica laughed. "I forgot the most important

thing. I forgot to buy the hamster!"

To the Store

By Sally Lucas

Illustrated by Pat Stewart

 Mother and Kirstin went to the garage

to get into the car. "Look," said Mother. "The

 car has a flat tire. How will we get to the  store?

We need bread, milk, and lots of potatoes."

"We can walk to the store," said Kirstin. "I'll

carry the bread, and you can carry the milk."

"But who will carry the potatoes?" asked Mother.

 Kirstin looked around the car in the garage.

"We can pull my wagon," said Kirstin. "My

 wagon can carry the bread, the milk, and

the potatoes."

"That is a good idea." Mother laughed.

"I know." Kirstin laughed, too. "My wagon never

gets a flat tire!"

18

Sleepy Uncle Hal

By Sally Lucas

Illustrated by Scott Sullivan

Uncle Hal moved into a house on a busy street. Every car that went by made noise. Every bus that went by made noise. Every truck that went by made noise. Every motorcycle that went by made noise. "Oh, dear," moaned Uncle Hal. "I can't sleep with all that noise."

One day Kate came to visit Uncle Hal. Kate liked the house on the busy street. Kate liked to watch every car, bus, truck, and motorcycle pass by. But Kate knew Uncle Hal could not sleep because of all the noise.

"Uncle Hal," said Kate, "I have a gift for you."

Every car that went by still made noise. So did every bus, truck, and motorcycle. But now Uncle Hal slept soundly. Kate was happy that he liked her gift—a pair of earmuffs!

Lunch Bag

By Sally Lucas

Illustrated by Jane Yamada

One morning Mike filled his lunch bag by himself. First Mike put in a sandwich. Next Mike put in some potato chips. Next Mike put in some cookies. Last of all Mike put in two big red apples. Then Mike got himself dressed and went to school.

At lunch Mike opened his lunch bag. What a mess! The sandwich was smashed. The potato chips were smashed. The cookies were smashed. "I'm glad the apples are OK," Mike said. "But next time I fill my lunch bag, the apples go on the bottom."

Grandma's Riddle

By Caroline Arnold
Illustrated by Olivia H. H. Cole

 Grandma had a basket of apples. She gave one to  Jenny.

 Jenny took a bite of the apple. It tasted good. "May we make a  pie with the apples?" Jenny asked.

"Yes," said Grandma. "But first I have a riddle for you. What is a little round house that is red and has a star in the middle?"

 Jenny thought hard. "Is it an apple?" she asked. "An apple is little and round and red. But I have never seen a star in the middle of an apple."

"Let me show you," said Grandma. She cut across the apple with a knife and opened it. The seeds inside made a perfect five-pointed star.

"Oh," said Jenny. "It *is* an apple!"

"Yes," said Grandma. "Now we can make our  apple pie."

The Mystery Can

By Lois Szymanski

Illustrated by Sal Murdocca

 Randy Raccoon shook the mystery can. It made a rackety, crackety rattle. The class sat still.

What is inside the 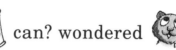 can? wondered Shirley Squirrel. Could it be a flower? No, a flower wouldn't rattle! Maybe stones, or seeds, or buttons?

If Shirley figured out what was in the can, she would win the game. Then she could take the can to her house and fill it with her own surprise. Shirley thought and thought. Suddenly she knew! She raised her paw.

 "Shirley," called Randy.

"Your favorite food is corn," said Shirley. "I think you have corn in the can."

 Randy laughed. He dumped out a pile of dried corn.

"Good guess!" he said as he handed the mystery  can to  Shirley.

What surprise do you think Shirley will hide in the can?

22

Guess What?

By Rosalyn Hart Finch

Illustrated by Meryl Henderson

"Guess what I am out of," 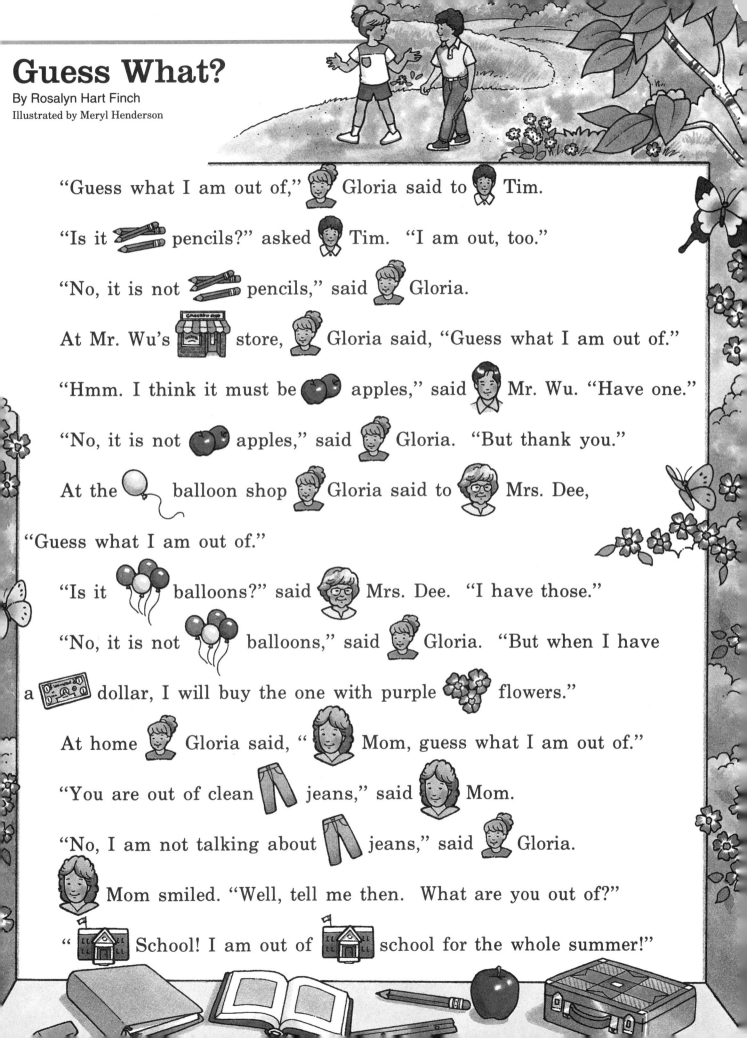 Gloria said to Tim.

"Is it pencils?" asked Tim. "I am out, too."

"No, it is not pencils," said Gloria.

At Mr. Wu's store, Gloria said, "Guess what I am out of."

"Hmm. I think it must be apples," said Mr. Wu. "Have one."

"No, it is not apples," said Gloria. "But thank you."

At the balloon shop Gloria said to Mrs. Dee,

"Guess what I am out of."

"Is it balloons?" said Mrs. Dee. "I have those."

"No, it is not balloons," said Gloria. "But when I have

a dollar, I will buy the one with purple flowers."

At home Gloria said, "Mom, guess what I am out of."

"You are out of clean jeans," said Mom.

"No, I am not talking about jeans," said Gloria.

Mom smiled. "Well, tell me then. What are you out of?"

"School! I am out of school for the whole summer!"

Bus Party

By Sally Lucas

Illustrated by Susan Parnell

One morning Betty carried a big box onto the school bus.

"Good morning," said Stan, the driver of the school bus. "What's in the box?"

"Look inside," said Betty.

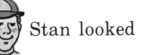 Stan looked inside the big box. " Cupcakes," Stan said. "I see chocolate cupcakes."

"The cupcakes are for you," said Betty.

Then all the children yelled, "Happy Birthday, Stan!"

"Thank you," said Stan. "Who wants to help me eat these yummy cupcakes?" Betty passed out the cupcakes. The children ate the cupcakes. Then they put the empty cupcake papers back in the big box.

"Thank you again," said  Stan. "You have given me

2 two birthday presents with **1** one box— cupcakes and a clean school bus!"

Pink Pig's Party

By Virginia Choo

Illustrated by Sue Parnell

Pink  Pig wanted to share his birthday cake. Pink Pig asked Red Rooster to come to his house. Pink Pig asked Orange Butterfly to come to his house. Pink Pig asked Blue Snake to come to his house. Pink Pig asked Green Turtle to come to his house.

Pink Pig waited for Red Rooster to come and ate one piece of cake. Pink Pig waited for Orange Butterfly to come and ate another piece of cake. Pink Pig waited for Blue Snake to come and ate another piece of cake. Pink Pig waited for Green Turtle to come and ate another piece of cake.

When Red Rooster and Orange Butterfly and Blue Snake and Green Turtle came to the party, there were birthday candles but no cake!

All the guests liked sharing the party fun, even if they could not share the cake.

Jody and the Clown

By Rosella J. Schroeder

Illustrated by
Olivia H.H. Cole

"I love the circus!" Jody said to her mother and father. She laughed and laughed as the clowns did their tricks. She watched the trapeze artist perform high above the crowd. Elephants marched one behind the other. Lions roared in their cages.

Jody was so busy watching, she did not see the clown standing by her.

"Come down," said the clown. "Be a clown, too."

He put a yellow wig and a round red nose on Jody.

The clown picked up a pail and threw water at Jody.

Jody laughed. "It's not water at all," she said. "It's just paper he threw at me."

She picked up some of the paper and ran after the clown.

When she caught up with him, she threw the paper at him.

The crowd laughed and cheered.

Circus Parade

By Sally Lucas

Illustrated by Roberta Collier

"Who will lead the parade inside the circus tent?"

asked the man with the whistle.

"I will," said the clown.

"I will," clapped the monkey.

"I will," nodded the elephant.

"Oh, dear," cried the man. "Which one of you

will I pick to lead the parade inside the circus tent?"

The clown smiled and whispered to

the elephant. The elephant stooped down.

Up went the clown and the monkey on top of

the elephant. The elephant stood up.

"Now blow your whistle," called the clown to

the man. "The elephant, monkey, and

I will lead the parade inside the circus tent!"

A Place for Everything

By Tamara Duncan

Illustrated by Susanne DeMarco

"Just look at this room!" Jonathan said to his little

brother,  Jeremy. "We need to clean up this mess. Our room

will stay neater if everything has a place."

 Jonathan lined up all the trucks on a  shelf.

He put all the blocks in a basket.

Then Jonathan placed all their shoes on the floor

of the closet and stacked all the  books on top of the

 dresser.

"I'm going downstairs to find a broom," Jonathan

told Jeremy. "I will be right back."

What a surprise Jonathan had when he came back

upstairs! The trucks, the blocks, the shoes, and

the books were all over the floor again!

"I know where I made my first mistake," sighed Jonathan.

"I should have found a place for Jeremy!"

Better Than a Robot

By Lanis Graunke

Illustrated by Sue Parnell

"I wish I had a robot," Paul said to his sister Christy.

"Why do you want a robot?" Christy asked.

"So the robot would pick up my blocks for me," Paul answered. "The robot could play ball with me and read books to me, too," Paul added. "It would be fun to watch a robot run around the house," said Paul.

"Hurry and finish cleaning up," Mother called.

"Too bad I do not have a robot," sighed Paul as he started putting away his blocks.

"I will help you pick up your blocks," said 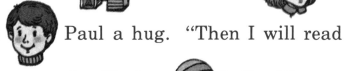 Christy as she ran over and gave Paul a hug. "Then I will read you a book, and tomorrow I will play ball with you."

"Thanks," said Paul happily. "You are better than a robot."

29

Soup or Salad?

By Eve Stone

Illustrated by Sal Murdocca

One day  Rabbit said, "I will make some soup for my friend Chipmunk." He went to his garden to pick some vegetables. He picked some carrots and put them in his wheelbarrow. He picked some tomatoes and put them in his wheelbarrow. He picked peppers and peas and potatoes and put them in his wheelbarrow.

Then Rabbit pushed his wheelbarrow down the path. He was so busy thinking about his soup that he did not notice the big hole in the path. The wheelbarrow hit the hole and tossed the vegetables into the air. They landed all over the garden.

Rabbit looked around. "Well, maybe Chipmunk would like tossed salad instead," he said as he gathered up the vegetables.

The Crow at the Well

Based on a Fable by Aesop   Retold by Jean K. Potratz
Illustrated by Jan Pyk

 Crow flew to a  pitcher sitting by a  well. "I need a drink," she said.

The  pitcher had only a little  water.  Crow tried to reach the  water. The  pitcher was too deep.

What could  Crow do? She was too small to fill the  pitcher with  water. How could  Crow get a drink?

 Crow looked around. The  trees could not help. The  grass could not help.  "Rocks!" crowed  Crow.

She picked up a small  rock in her  beak. She dropped the  rock into the  pitcher.  Crow dropped more and more  rocks into the  pitcher. The  water rose higher and higher.

Finally  Crow could reach the  water in the  pitcher. Happily, she drank her fill.

A Small Red Truck

By Judith Ross Enderle

Illustrated by Jerry Weisman

 Lottie looked down. She saw a small red truck in the tall

 grass. She picked up the truck.

"Good," said Lottie. "Now I have a nice red truck for my

 sandbox." She put the truck in her pocket.

Later, Lottie met Janet. She looked very sad. "I have lost

my  truck. Will you help me look for it?" Janet said.

"Yes," said Lottie. "What does it look like?"

"It is red and it fits in my hand," said Janet.

 Lottie wished Janet had lost a green car instead.

She took the  truck from her pocket. "I found your

 truck," she said. "I did not know it was yours."

 Janet looked happy. "It is my favorite truck," she said.

"It is a pretty color," said Lottie.

"I will let you play with my little red truck," said Janet.

"We can play in my sandbox," said Lottie.

Playing with Janet's truck was almost as good as having it for her

own. Lottie felt good inside.

32

Ben and the Big Ball

By Anita Wagner

Illustrated by Joy Friedman

 Ben walked to the park with his mother. Ben had his big ball with him.

Carrying his ball, Ben ran to the swings. All of them were taken, but none of his friends were there.

 Ben ran to the slide. No friends there either.

Slowly, Ben walked to the sandbox. It was empty.

"I don't have anyone to play with," he said sadly.

 Ben sat in the middle of the sandbox. He put his ball next to him on the sand. The wind blew the ball out of the sandbox and across the park.

"Help!" Ben shouted. "Help me catch my ball."

 Children came from all over the park. They ran after the ball. Finally they caught it.

"This is fun," the children shouted.

 Ben threw the ball and the children chased it again. Ben laughed as he ran with the children.

City Letter, Country Letter

By Richard Hohl

Illustrated by Meryl Henderson

 Mother helped Ted write a letter. "Dear  Uncle Bill, Thanks for inviting me to the farm. Mother said I can come on the airplane. Love, Ted." Ted put the letter in the mailbox on the corner. "Now Uncle Bill will get my  letter."

A week later Uncle Bill was waiting when Ted got off the airplane. When they reached the farm, Ted said, "I want to write Mother a letter." With Uncle Bill's help, he wrote, "Dear Mother, The ride on the airplane was fun. Tomorrow I am going to help on the farm. Thanks for letting me visit Uncle Bill. Love, Ted."

 Uncle Bill and Ted walked to the mailbox by the road. Ted put the  letter in the  mailbox. Then he reached high and put up the red flag, so the mail carrier would stop. "Now Mother will get my letter," he said. "It's fun to send mail."

34

Buddy's Letter

By Pat Kite

Illustrated by Lorraine Arthur

"I want to write a letter," said Buddy.

"Here's some paper and a pencil," said

Mother. "But who will you write to?"

Buddy thought a moment. "I will write to my

teacher, Mrs. Brent," he decided. "I will tell her

that it is fun being in her class."

Buddy picked up the pencil. He wrote

very carefully. Mother gave him an

 envelope and a stamp. Buddy

licked the stamp and stuck it on the envelope.

Then Mother helped him write the address.

"I think that Mrs. Brent will be happy to get

my letter," said Buddy. He was happy, too.

The Little Sea Gull

By Sally Lucas

Illustrated by Ethel Gold

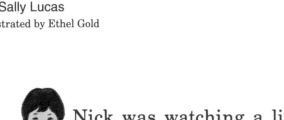

 Nick was watching a little sea gull on the  sand.

The little sea gull stood by a 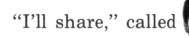 woman who was catching

a fish. The  woman put the  fish into a bucket.

She did not share her fish with the little sea gull.

The little sea gull flew to a man who was buying a

hot dog. The man began to eat the hot dog. He did

not share his hot dog with the little sea gull.

"I'll share," called Nick. He reached into his basket

and took out a piece of bread. *Scree! Scree!* Many big

sea gulls crowded around Nick. The little sea gull

could not get close to him.

Nick tossed the piece of bread as high as he could

into the air. Swish! The little sea gull flew up and caught the

bread in mid-air.

"Good catch," cried Nick.

An Ocean for Ben

By Herma Silverstein
Illustrated by Allan Eitzen

 Ben was digging a hole in the sand when his

shovel hit something hard. Ben looked into the hole.

He pulled out a  shell.

"It is beautiful," Mother said.

"The shell is sandy," said Ben. "I will wash it

in the waves."

When he finished, Mother said, "It is time to leave."

 Ben frowned and said to Mother, "I wish we

could stay here forever. I will miss the beach."

"Sometimes people take something home to remember the place

they visited," 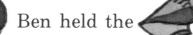 Mother said. " Ben, hold the

 shell against your ear."

 Ben held the shell to his ear. "It sounds like

waves," he shouted. "I hear the ocean in my shell!"

 Ben smiled. "I cannot swim in the waves at

home, but I can still hear them. I will hold my shell and

listen to my special ocean."

Little Brother

By Caroline Arnold
Illustrated by Lorraine Arthur

Simon waved good-bye to his brother, Greg.

Then the bus drove away. Simon said, "I wish

I could go to school."

"You will when you are 5 five," Mother told him.

Simon rode his tricycle up the driveway.

"I wish I had a two-wheel bike," Simon said.

Greg had a two-wheel bike in the garage.

"You will when you are bigger," Mother said to

him. "But now I want you to come into the house. I

need your help. We are going to bake bread."

"Goody," Simon said. He liked fresh, homemade

bread. And he knew that Mother always gave

her helper the first piece.

Sometimes it was nice to be younger than Greg.

Nursery School

By Sally Lucas

Illustrated by Lorraine Arthur

It was the first day of nursery school. Karen looked

around the room at all the  toys.

She saw a big box of blocks. She saw a big

 box of trucks. She saw a big box of

 books and crayons.

"Snack time," called the teacher. Karen ran to a

 table and sat down on a chair. She had

 cookies and a glass of milk.

 Mother came into the nursery school. "It is time to go

home," she said.

"Time to go home?" asked Karen. "But I just got here."

"I know," said Mother. "This was just a visiting time.

Tomorrow you can spend all day."

"That is good," said  Karen. "It will take me all day

to play with all the  toys."

Baking Ice Skates

By Stephanie Moody

Illustrated by Meryl Henderson

Baked goods for sale

If you're hungry, follow me

"I wish I had ice skates," Mike said as he watched skaters gliding on the frozen pond.

"Me too," said Mother. "Why don't we bake some today?"

 Mike and Mother worked all day. Together they mixed flour and sugar and eggs and milk. Into the oven went the dough. Out of the oven came cookies and  cakes and brownies. But no ice skates.

"Soon," said Mother. "Just take this sign down to the pond." The sign said: Baked goods for sale. If you're hungry, follow me.

All of the skaters followed Mike to his house. Into a shoebox went nickels and dimes and quarters. Out of the kitchen went cookies and cakes and brownies.

Soon Mike's kitchen was empty, but the shoebox was full.

"For ice skates," said Mother, lifting the shoebox.

"Wow!" said Mike. "Tomorrow can we bake an elephant?"

Rainy-Day Snowman

by Marilyn Kratz

Illustrated by Olivia H.H. Cole

"I wish we lived where it snows," said Cathy, looking out at the rainy day.

"Me too," said Joan. "We cannot even make a snowman."

"A rainy day is a good day to make a snowman," said Father.

"How can we make a snowman without snow?" asked Cathy.

"First, you must make some popcorn," said Father.

While the girls did that, Father cooked a sticky syrup. He poured it over the popcorn.

"Now butter your hands," said Father. "We will make 3 three popcorn balls--a big one, a middle-sized one, and a small one."

Next, they stacked the balls on top of each other, like a snowman. Father gave the girls some gumdrops to make the eyes and mouth.

Cathy nibbled a bit of the sweet popcorn. "I like a rainy day snowman better than a real one," she said.

Garden Surprise

By Carolyn Breecher

Illustrated by Morissa Lipstein

 Judy talked to Grandpa on the telephone.

"Tomorrow I will bring you a surprise from my  garden," said  Grandpa.

"Is it 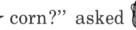 corn?" asked Judy.

"No," said  Grandpa. "My surprise is round."

"Maybe it is a tomato," said 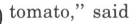 Judy.

"It is bigger than a tomato," said  Grandpa.

"Can it be a watermelon?" asked Judy.

"It is as big as a watermelon," said 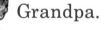 Grandpa. "But it is orange."

 Judy thought. "It grows in your  garden. It is big and round and orange. Oh! Can we make it into a

 jack-o'-lantern?"

"Yes," said Grandpa.

Next day Grandpa brought the surprise. It was a big, round, orange pumpkin.

You Can't Trick Tracy

By Mike Carter

Illustrated by Ethel Gold

Tracy's  father peeked out the front window.

 "Tracy!" he yelled. "There's a pirate walking down

the sidewalk in front of our house."

"You're not going to trick me tonight, Daddy!" said Tracy.

"I'm serious," he said. "And she's talking to a 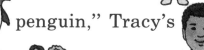 caveman."

"That's nice," said  Tracy, yawning.

"Now I see an  astronaut holding hands with a

 penguin," Tracy's father added. "They're being joined by

two mermaids. And now . . . Oh no . . ."

"Now what?" said Tracy.

"They're walking up to our  house."

Just then there was a knock at the door.

"Don't open the door!" Tracy's father warned.

"Don't be silly, Daddy," said Tracy as she opened

the door. Well, there they were. A pirate, a caveman,

an astronaut, a penguin, and two mermaids.

"Trick or treat!" they shouted.

The Snowman and the Scarecrow

By Ruth A. Sakri

Illustrated by Jan Pyk

Said the  snowman to the scarecrow,

"You are wearing ragged clothes,

And you're made of straw and branches,

And your job is chasing crows."

Snowman said, "I'm made of snowflakes,

And I sparkle like a ring.

I am dressed in gloves and top hat,

And in winter I am king."

Said the scarecrow to the snowman,

"Yes. I'm only made of straw,

But I'll still have clothes and branches

When your snowflakes

start

to

thaw."

Follow That Carrot

By Herma Steen

Illustrated by Sue Parnell

"Time to dress the  snowman," said Jane.

 Father lifted Jane up. She put the hat and scarf on the snowman.

"Where is the 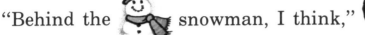 carrot for the nose?" Jane asked.

"Behind the snowman, I think," Father said.

 Jane and Father walked behind the snowman. "I do not see the carrot," Jane said. "But I see paw tracks."

 Father and Jane followed the paw tracks to the porch. Jane looked under the porch. She saw a rabbit eating the carrot.

 Father said, "The rabbit is hungry. In the winter it is hard for a rabbit to find food."

Quickly,  Jane ran into the 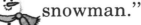 house. She brought back two carrots.

"Look, Father," said Jane. "One for the rabbit and one for the snowman."

Patient Sarah

By Stephanie Gordon Tessler

Illustrated by Morissa Lipstein

"When will Hanukkah come?" asked Sarah.

"You must be patient," Father said.

"I will make  stars with six points. When Hanukkah comes, I will hang up my stars," Sarah said.

Sarah waited and waited. "Is it Hanukkah yet?" she asked.

"Not yet. You must be patient," answered Mother.

So Sarah waited. She polished the brass menorah for the Hanukkah candles. She tried to be patient.

One day Mother baked star cookies. She put blue frosting on all the star cookies.

Father brought home a box of colorful twisted candles. He gave Sarah a new red dreidel to spin.

"We have star cookies with six points. We have twisted candles. And I have a new dreidel to spin. Now it is Hanukkah," Sarah said.

She clapped her hands. "Happy Hanukkah, everybody."

46

A Special Tree

By Rosella J. Schroeder

Illustrated by Roberta Collier

"Come and see what I have," said Daddy.

"But we already have a Christmas tree," said Mark.

"This is a special tree," said Daddy. "Go get the popcorn and cranberries you were stringing."

Mark and Daddy hung strings of popcorn and cranberries. They sprinkled birdseed on the ground.

Later Mark saw red cardinals, little chickadees, and a blue jay in the branches. Finches fed on the ground along with a rabbit and a squirrel.

"Come and look, Daddy. It really is a special tree," said Mark. "The birds in the branches are like ornaments. And the finches, the squirrel, and the rabbit are like presents. We decorated the tree for the animals. Now they are decorating it for us!"

Nathan's Nest

By Lora Olson
Illustrated by Ethel Gold

The cold wind blew and blew. "Brrr," said Chipmunk. Chipmunk dug a hole in the ground. She carried grass into the hole and piled it into a nest. When she was done, she curled up in the nest and fell asleep. Chipmunk slept most of the winter.

"Brrr," said Bear. Bear made a pile of leaves and twigs in a cave. When he was done, he lay down on the leaves and twigs and fell asleep. Bear slept most of the winter.

"Brrr," said Nathan. Nathan made a big pile of blankets on his bed. When he was done, he climbed under the blankets. "I am going to sleep all winter," he said. But Nathan woke up just in time for breakfast.